for Tom

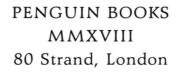

PENGUIN BOOKS
MMXVIII
80 Strand, London

The Worm
and
the Bird

Coralie
Bickford-Smith

There's
not
much
room
where
I live

and all
the earth
around me
is filled
with life

I am
always
searching
for space,

and
everything
is in
my way.

I am
too
busy
to
rest,

I can
rest
later.

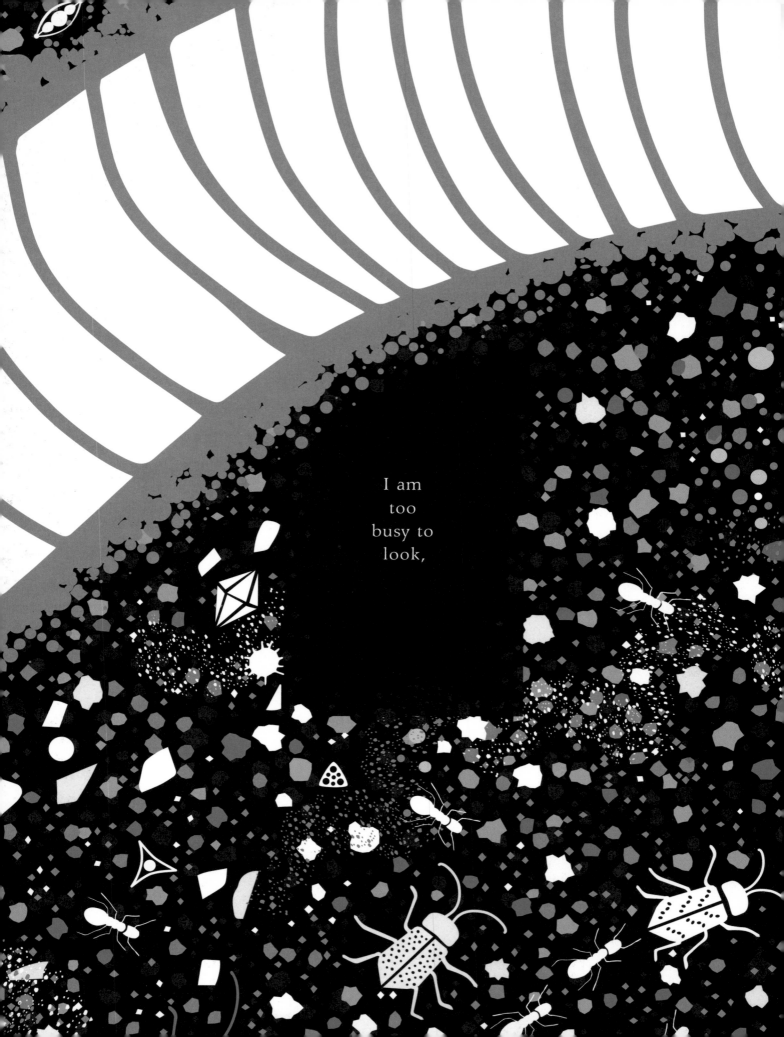

I am
too
busy to
look,

I can
look
another
day.

I am
too
busy
to
listen,

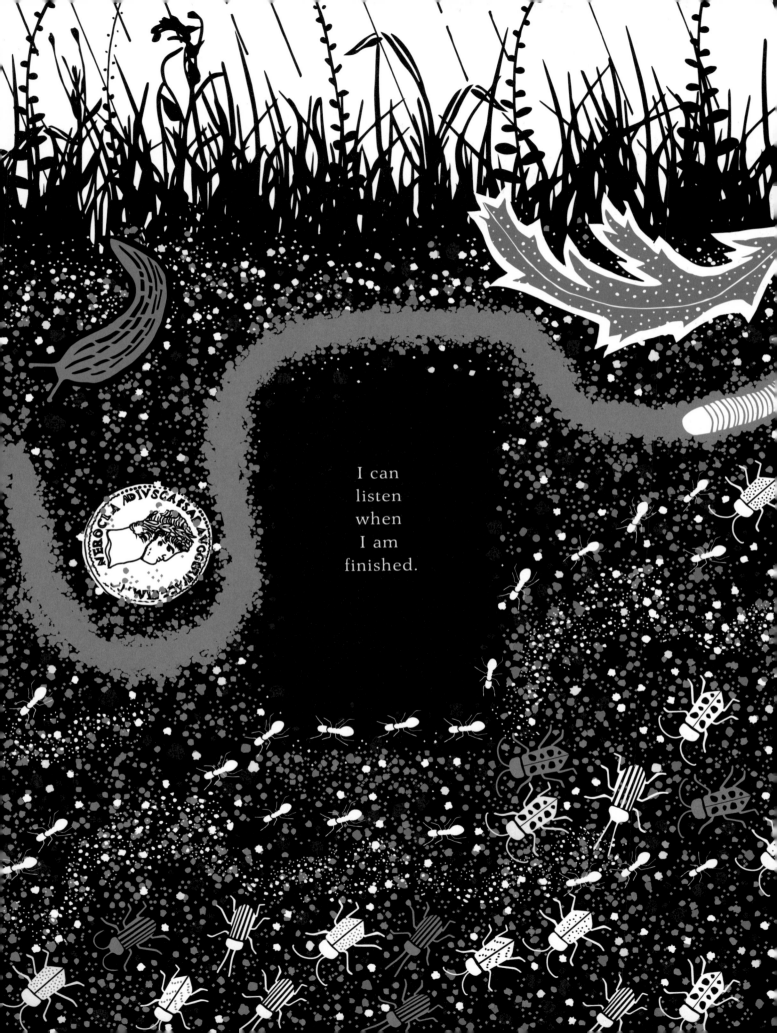

I can
listen
when
I am
finished.

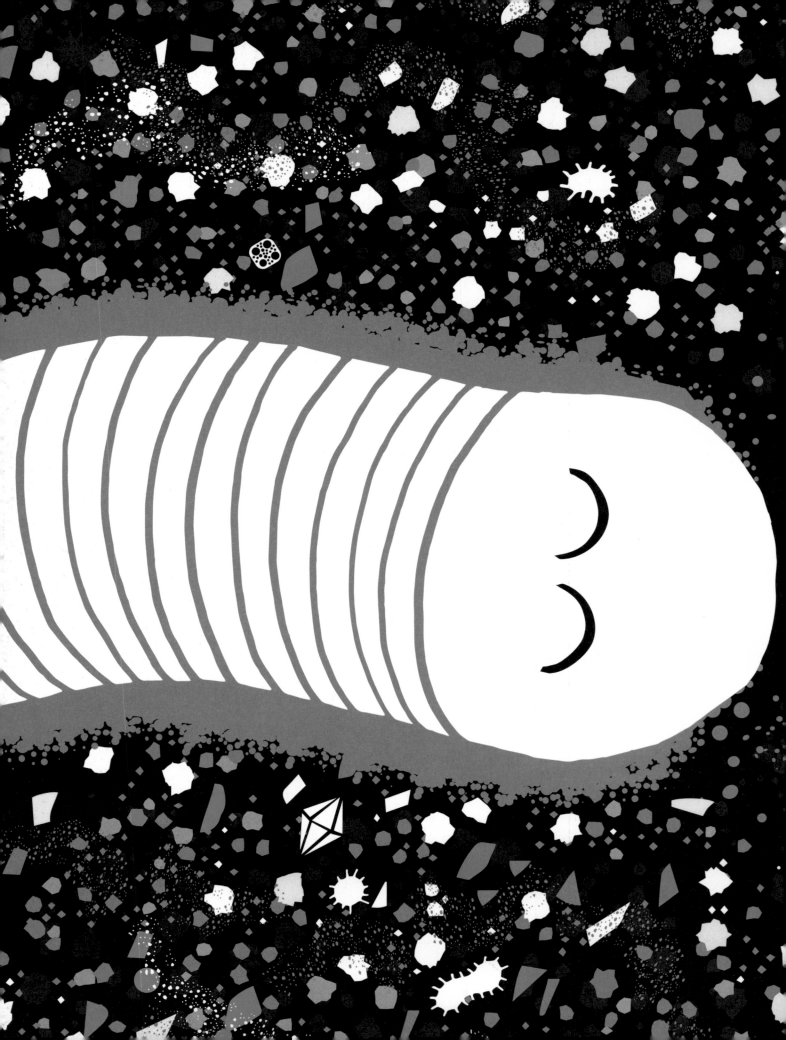

But
I dream
of a place.

A space
with
nothing.

A place
where
I can be
truly
alone.

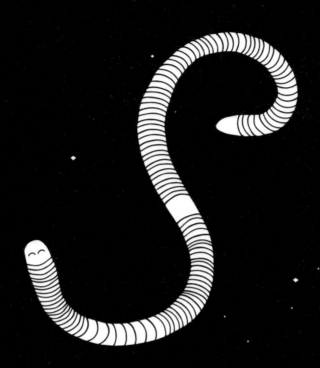

Today!

Today
is the day!

I will push everything

out of

my way . . .

I am

getting

really

good

at

this . . .

I see
Earth!

It is so
beautiful!

There's

not

much

room

where

I live

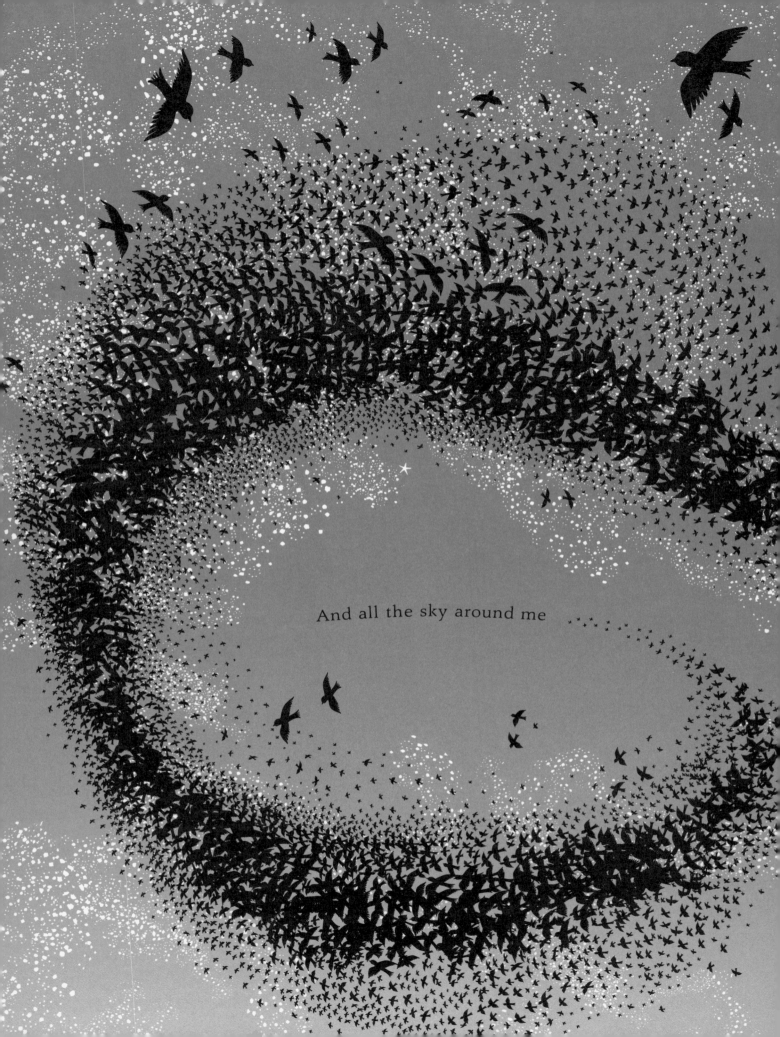

And all the sky around me

is filled with life